THE STRANGE AND
EXCITING ADVENTURES OF
# JEREMIAH HUSH

Jeremiah Hush

*The*
STRANGE
*and* EXCITING
ADVENTURES *of*

# *Jeremiah Hush*

AS TOLD FOR THE BENEFIT
OF ALL PERSONS OF GOOD SENSE
AND RECORDED TO THE BEST OF
HIS LIMITED ABILITY BY

## URI SHULEVITZ

AND VOUCHED FOR AS TO
THEIR CERTAINTY BY

*Jeremiah Hush*
HIMSELF

*Farrar · Straus · Giroux*
NEW YORK

*To the memory of my mother*
*With thanks to P.S.B.*

THE STRANGE AND
EXCITING ADVENTURES OF
# JEREMIAH HUSH

# Certificate of Approval

THIS IS
TO CERTIFY THAT I,
JEREMIAH HUSH, HAVE
CAREFULLY READ AND INSPECTED
THE STORIES THAT FOLLOW, AND
APPROVE, AND ENDORSE, AND
RECOMMEND THEM, AND CONFIRM
THAT THEY REPRESENT A
FAITHFUL PORTRAIT OF MY TRUE
SELF AND OF THE EVENTS THE
WAY THEY HAPPENED

*Jeremiah Hush*

# *Jeremiah Hush*
# *Goes to Town*

BEING A
DETAILED ACCOUNT
OF THE GOINGS AND COMINGS OF
JEREMIAH HUSH AND OF HIS
EXTRAORDINARY ADVENTURES
IN ORANGUTANVILLE

( In another solar system, on a strange planet curiously resembling our own, there lived (and still lives) a middle-aged monkey known as Jeremiah Hush. He was a quiet and serious fellow, young at heart and youthful in appearance. He lived alone in a small house surrounded by trees and fields, and was content to be by himself in an out-of-the-way spot and grow vegetables in his little garden. During the day he loved to listen to birds singing duets on tree branches, and at night to cricket orchestras in the grass and to frog ensembles by the pond.

Jeremiah Hush was a poet at heart, though he never wrote a line of poetry.

He was a reasonably happy monkey. That is, he was usually happy: when he worked in his garden, when he watched his vegetables grow or the frogs dance, or when he listened to the music of the birds and crickets. But sometimes he did nothing in particular and his mind wandered. Then he began to think about what others might be doing at that very moment. And the more he thought about it, the more he was convinced that they were having the time of their lives. They were probably having fun—an elusive, indescribable, sort of fun. And he would worry that something might be missing in his own life. Something . . . something . . . he wasn't quite sure what. And when he worried, his happiness vanished. Instantly he felt twelve years and four and a half months older, his head three ounces heavier, and his nose almost three eighths of an inch longer.

❦ One day Jeremiah Hush read in *The Bi-Monthly Banana Leaf* about the Shake'n'Roll Dancin' Hole. According to the story in *The Leaf*, it was the last

word in dancing the wiggle-waggle and in shake'n' roll music. Everyone interviewed was ecstatic. They highly praised the exquisite music, the exotic dances, and the enchanting atmosphere of the place. They could hardly find words fit to describe its endless wonders and fantastic fun. To make a long story short, the Shake'n'Roll Dancin' Hole was the best thing since marinated mangoes, and possibly the three thousand seven hundred fifty-sixth wonder of Orangutanville County.

The wiggle-waggle might be it, thought our hero, impressed by the story. "The very thing I've been missing." From that day on, the Shake'n'Roll Dancin' Hole and the wiggle-waggle occupied a prominent place in his thoughts. Gradually, they began to fill up every available space in his dreams as well. And thus, being preoccupied day and night with misty visions of dancing the wiggle-waggle, he had no time to think or to do anything else. As time went on, he enjoyed his house less and less. He didn't enjoy working in his garden either, or listening to birds singing duets on tree branches, cricket orchestras in the grass, or frog ensembles by the pond.

"Here I am," he complained, "in an out-of-the-way spot, forgotten by the world, neglected by everybody, denied my share of life's swect raisins, and all the fun is skipping by me."

He had an irresistible longing to dance the wiggle-waggle, and nothing else would do. He had never wiggle-waggled before, but never mind that. Also, he had to find someone to dance with, but surely he could. And though he felt scared, his desire to go to the Shake'n'Roll Dancin' Hole won out.

He put on his double-breasted jacket, striped pants, wide necktie with magnolia flowers, and his old pointed dancing shoes.

"By my great-grandfather's whiskers," he said, surveying his likeness in the mirror, "you look pretty smart."

⟨ In no time he reached the outskirts of Orangutanville.

As he got closer to the center of town, there were more and more autodrivemobiles. Soon there were so many that he had to drive at a snail's pace. Jeremiah was anxious to get there. Impatiently, he looked around. In the neighboring autodrivemobiles he saw couples all dressed up, going to dance the wiggle-waggle, no doubt. After all, this was the great night out.

Finally, when he reached the Shake'n'Roll Dancin' Hole, there was a long line at the entrance. Everybody was dressed in what was absolutely the last word in fashion: Michel Giraffé straight-tight jackets; André Saint d'Elephanté baggy trousers with green, broken-glass patterns; Ricardo von Alligatori's skinny neckties with bent, rusty-nail designs; and square-toed shoes with high soles. Jeremiah Hush felt silly in his old-fashioned clothes, and was greatly relieved to observe that nobody paid attention to his pointed shoes.

"Two and a half bananas," announced the door attendant, looking down his beak, "admission fee." Then he stamped the ticket on Jeremiah Hush's forehead. "Invisible ink," he explained to our surprised hero. "Now you may enter or leave as you please."

The renowned Shake'n'Roll Dancin' Hole was packed like the proverbial jar of pickled scallions, and filled with smoke thick enough to be cut with a knife and fork. Ear-deafening noise, faintly resembling music, and countless blinding, blinking traffic lights for special effect and atmosphere completed the picture.

Jeremiah Hush was afraid that the place was on fire. But everybody behaved as if things had never been better. Little smoking chimneys of varying lengths were in almost everyone's mouth or hand.

Our hero's eyes began to burn and his throat became dry. He battled his way toward the bottlebar. After what seemed an endless and sometimes hopeless struggle, he reached the bar, where many shake'n'rollers were perched on high stools, sipping brownish drinks in tall glasses. He managed to find an unoccupied stool and climbed on top. It took a good while to get the bottletender's attention and order something to drink. The bottletender pushed a tall glass of brownish liquid toward Jeremiah. It almost landed in his lap. "That'll be two bananas and six peanuts," he shouted above the noise.

"Expensive," mumbled Jeremiah Hush under his breath, as he put down two bananas and six peanuts, and an additional four peanuts for the bottletender's efforts in pushing the glass, and in gratitude for his not spilling the drink.

"Yes, sir," said a grave-looking hippo next to him knowingly, "you need loads of bananas here."

By now Jeremiah Hush's throat was as dry as desert dust.

He took a gulp of his drink, wrinkled his nose, and almost fell off the stool. The drink tasted like cider vinegar spiced with generous amounts of hot red pepper. When he recovered from the shock, he glanced around: everybody else was drinking it with a straight face.

"Yes, sir, the spice of life, the very thing," commented the hippo, as he took another sip of "the very thing." "Pure spice of life," he repeated with emphasis, which inspired our hero to give the drink another chance. He took a sip cautiously, but it was no use; it tasted worse than ever. "A hopeless drink," he decided.

❪Now a band of musicians, with an assortment of musical gourds, three automatic water hoses, and five electric watermelons, jumped on stage. Their leader, a tall owl with pumpernickel-brown eyeglasses, exclaimed, "Babbledee gobblede *gook*!

Brambledegrumbledee *go*! Go go go *go*! Hoo! hoo! hoo! *hoo*! Ha ha ha *haaa*!!!" And suddenly there was an explosion of ear-piercing music, full of hoo-hoo-hoo-hoos and ha-ha-ha-has. All around Jeremiah Hush animals groaned with delight. Nearby, a sensitive-looking turtle with a heavy sweater and a sports jacket with oil paint spots was sweating profusely. "This is almost a transmegamystical experience," he mumbled in a state of near ecstasy. The musicians wiggled and waggled to the beat of the music, wobbled and shook, faster and faster. They sang, "Boo-boo-de-*boo*! Goo-goo-de-*goo*! Da-da-de-*doo*! Hoo-hoo-de-*hoo*!" The owl began chewing the microphone and the musicians eating their instruments in a frenzy. The legendary Shake'n'Roll Dancin' Hole shook from ceiling to floor. Everybody went wild.

When things calmed down a bit, many began dancing. Ah, thought Jeremiah Hush, the wiggle-waggle, at last. They were hopping and skipping, shaking and rolling, wiggling and waggling. Some danced nose to nose.

The wiggle-waggle of my dreams, thought Jeremiah, as he strained to watch the dancers through

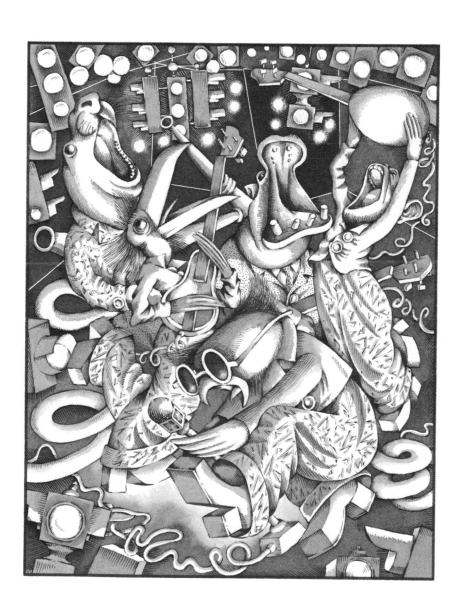

the thick smoke. He didn't know how to dance it, but it seemed easy enough.

He looked around and saw a kangaroo sitting alone, staring into her glass. Bravely he walked over. "May I have this dance?" he asked politely. Without taking her eyes off her glass, she replied, "I don't feel like it." Jeremiah, mildly disappointed, returned to his place at the counter.

I mustn't give up too easily, he encouraged himself. He walked over to a slim giraffe, sitting by herself and watching everyone dance. "May I have this dance?" he asked. Finally, after a long, and no doubt meaningful, silence, she said, without even looking at him, "Sorry, I'm busy right now."

*Giraffe me no giraffes*, he thought somewhat angrily, as he walked away.


This place sounded so much better when I read about it in *The Leaf*, he thought as he turned toward the exit.

Then he reminded himself, After all the trouble it took to come here, I mustn't give up so easily. I'll give it one more try.

And lo and behold, next to him, as if brought by

providence, was an elegant ostrich. "May I have this dance?" he inquired. She took a quick glance at him from the corner of her eye, said, "Look at those shoes," and walked away.

Jeremiah was stunned.

Then, suddenly he felt very lonely.

He decided to leave.


¶ Exhausted, his eyes burning, Jeremiah battled through the crowd back to the exit, where he saw the hippo again.

"Having fun?" Jeremiah shouted above the noise.

"Who, me?" the hippo yelled back in surprise.

"Why come, then?"

"Nothing better to do. Did you have fun?"

"No," said Jeremiah. "This is not my cup of cocoa."

"Take care," said the hippo.

"You, too, my friend."


¶ Outside, the fresh air was delicious. "*Oh, sweet taste of life!* Am I glad to get out of that madhouse. I can't wait to get away," Jeremiah said to himself.

But his autodrivemobile wouldn't start.

He went to look for a teleblablaphone to call an autodrivemobile mechanic. The first teleblablaphone booth didn't have an Orangutanville directory, and the second telcblablaphone was out of order. He had to look for a third to make his call to the Alert and Dependable Autodrivemobile Repair Service.

An hour later, the mechanic, a half-asleep sloth, arrived, only to announce in a soft voice, "By sixty-seven scratchy screeking alarm clocks, I brought the wrong tools," and he left.

But he was back later with a battery-operated stethoscope and an air-powered tapping hammer. "By seventy-seven screeching roosters, I'm ready," he declared. He listened to the silent engine, sniffed around, blew his nose carefully, yawned, blinked his eyes four times to keep awake, tapped in the middle of the trouble spot eight times, and the autodrivemobile started. He gave Jeremiah the bill for his professional services: two bananas for listening with the stethoscope, two bananas and eight peanuts for sniffing at the appropriate place, sixteen peanuts (two per tap) for tapping, ten peanuts for waking him up, minus a two-peanut discount for forgetting to bring the right tools. After Jeremiah paid his bill, he had one banana left.

"By seven thousand seven hundred seventy-seven soundly snoring sleepy sloths," said the sloth before leaving, "why, for heaven's sake, be up so late?"

"I went to the Shake'n'Roll Dancin' Hole," explained Jeremiah Hush.

"So sorry, sport," spoke the sloth slowly, interrupting his speech with several yawns. "So you went to that sleep-spoiling spot, eh? My special sympathies, you poor soul. Serves you swell. I'd sooner snooze anytime."

( And so, finally, our hero left Orangutanville and slowly drove on the deserted road back to his house. When he got home, he sat down outside. He felt sad about his evening. He looked at his old pointed dancing shoes, shook his head, and said to himself, *Clothes do not make the monkey.* Then he looked up. A full moon shone overhead. It seemed to smile sympathetically at him. He

heard the sounds of a few crickets and frogs not
yet retired for their morning naps. Sweet music of
the night, thought Jeremiah Hush, for he was a
poet at heart.

Then he went inside and took a hot bath to
cleanse himself of all the smoke from the Shake'n'-
Roll Dancin' Hole. When he came out again, he
declared to the moon, "Why *monkey* around with
someone who doesn't want to *ostrich* with me?"
and began to dance. It was a dance after his own
heart. At first, slowly and gently, then faster and
faster, he danced as he felt, and danced as it came,
until he was out of breath.

Then, to celebrate his return home and to his
senses, he boiled some milk and made a cup of hot
cocoa, just the way he liked it, sweetened with
honey and a dash of cinnamon. He sat down by the
window and drank it slowly, savoring every sip.

Never mind what others might be doing, he
decided. If something is missing in my life, it
certainly is not the Shake'n'Roll Dancin' Hole.
And with that, he ate his last banana.

Tomorrow I've got a busy day, he thought. My
garden needs me.

He yawned, and went to bed.

Between the half-drawn window shades, pale, golden streaks of light were gently streaming in. On a nearby tree, two birds were beginning to sing.

# Jeremiah Hush Goes in Search of His Umbrella

BEING THE
FAITHFUL ACCOUNT OF
THE WAY JEREMIAH HUSH
INVESTIGATES THE MYSTERIOUS
DISAPPEARANCE OF HIS UMBRELLA,
AND HOW THE INVESTIGATION
REVEALS THAT HE DOESN'T
KNOW HIS OWN HOUSE, AND
NEIGHBORS HE DOESN'T
KNOW HE HAS

When Jeremiah Hush woke up, he knew right away that this was a morning for sour-milk, buckwheat pancakes.

While raindrops streamed down the windowpanes, the kitchen filled with appetizing smells. Jeremiah Hush sat at his table, facing seven thick, steaming pancakes piled high on a plate, topped with blueberries and sour cream and pure maple syrup.

After he had cleaned off his plate, savoring every bite, he thought, What can be worthy of such a fine beginning? Hmm, a cup of cocoa will go well with pancakes on a rainy day.

Hah, he thought further, I always do the same thing, creature of habit that I am. Why not do something *different* for a change?

He got up and paced the kitchen four times, back and forth, thinking hard.

Something different . . . something different . . . something . . . cocoa by the pond? Why not? Why not watch raindrops forming rings in the water? Of course!

He prepared the cocoa and poured it steaming hot into a container, placed it in a picnic basket, and then put on his red rubber boots, yellow raincoat, and orange hat. All he needed was his umbrella, to protect the picnic basket from the rain. But he couldn't find it.

Where in the world is my umbrella? he said to himself, looking everywhere.

He searched for his umbrella where he sometimes left it. He searched where he seldom left it. Then he searched where he never left it, just in case he had left it there. Nothing. No umbrella in sight. He was frustrated.

Did I forget it somewhere? He thought very hard, sitting in his soft chair in the living room. No. Last time I had it, I brought it home to dry. But where is it?

He searched all over again. Nothing.

By the time he gave up searching, he had given up going to the pond as well. Disappointed, he drank the cold cocoa and stared at the rivulets streaming down the windowpanes.

Suddenly it hit him. "*Someone must have taken it!*"

An invasion of his house, an intrusion into his home, was more than he could bear.


Jeremiah Hush dialed the Orangutanville County Watchdog Security Office. "There has been an intrusion into my home," he told them, "and my umbrella has been stolen."

The officer on duty promised they would be there at nine-thirty sharp, without fail.

An Orangutanville County Watchdog Security Office autodrivemobile pulled up in front of Jeremiah Hush's house at precisely eleven-forty-six. Three officers—Sergeant Moose, Patrolman Pekingese, and Detective Raccoon—asked endless questions concerning the strange disappearance of Jeremiah Hush's umbrella, to which he responded with all the available details. Then they held a conference in the vestibule while our hero waited anxiously in the living room.

"It looks like your umbrella has been taken without your knowledge or permission," said Sergeant Moose to Jeremiah Hush. "We sympathize with you. It's disturbing when you can't tell what's happening in your own house."

"I'm so glad you understand," said Jeremiah Hush. "You see, it isn't just the umbrella, it is the intrusion into my home that disturbs me."

"Interesting case," said the detective to the patrolman. "No sign of forced entry."

"Puzzling, very puzzling," replied the patrolman. "A mystery, if you ask me. I don't understand it at all."

"We would like to help you," said Sergeant Moose.

"Oh, thank you," said Jeremiah Hush.

"But we can't," said the sergeant.

"Why not?"

"We can only follow the rules. And the rules are that if it doesn't walk, or run, or fly, or crawl, or roll, or otherwise move by itself, or if it exceeds ten and one-eighth inches in length, but is shorter than seven feet and three inches, or is valued at less than three bananas and four peanuts, or is too small, or too large, or too narrow, or too wide, or . . . or . . . or . . ."

"Orchid four-oh-four, Orchid four-oh-four, ordering patrol autodrivemobile six-forty-eight-and-a-half ordinary report to Orbit seven-eight-five, Orchard Hill and Oregano Organization. Check if all is orderly. Over," said a voice coming from the sergeant's pocket.

"Six-forty-eight-and-a-half ordinary, that's us.

Coming over. Over," said the sergeant to his pocket.

"Pardon me, what's that?" asked our puzzled hero.

"That's my walkie-talkie," said the sergeant. "As for your umbrella, it is outside our jurisdiction. Our hands are tied. The law's the law."

"Is there anything at all you can do?" asked Jeremiah Hush.

"I'm afraid not," said Sergeant Moose. "Sorry." And he left.

"Sorry," said the detective, and he followed the sergeant.

"Sorry," said the patrolman, and then he whispered, "I'm not supposed to do this, but a very distant relative of mine is a private investigator. Here's his card. For a very distant relative, he's pretty good." And he rushed out to catch up with the others.


❲ Left on his own, Jeremiah Hush looked at the card. It said:

WINCHESTER BONE, P.I., E.P.E., INC.
*By appointment only. Tel. ORA 3–0004*

and in small letters:

> *Strictly confidential. Satisfaction guaranteed*
> *Affordable fees and prompt service*
> *Large or small jobs. No offer turned down*

Has a friendly ring to it, thought Jeremiah Hush, when he finished reading it. Why not try him?

He walked over to his teleblablaphone and called. A recording machine answered, so he left a message. About three days later, Winchester Bone in person returned his call and promised to arrive in the late afternoon of the following day.

Indeed, a small, beat-up autodrivemobile with a big black trunk tied with ropes to its roof rack pulled up in front of our hero's house, late in the afternoon of the promised day. A heavyset dog with a large mustache and a milk bone stuck in the corner of his mouth was driving. He opened the door slowly and got out of the autodrivemobile with great difficulty. He wore dark glasses, a large black top hat, and a long cape sprinkled with nondescript stains. He approached Jeremiah Hush slowly, leaning on his cane, and walking as if he were stepping on shaky ground.

"Jeremiah Hush, I presume," he announced in a youthful voice. "Greetings. I'm Winchester Bone, Private Investigator, Extraordinary Par Excellence, of Winchester Bone, Inc. Proprietor, president, investigator-in-chief," and in a lower voice, "Secretary, clerk, and receptionist. At your service." He took off his top hat, revealing a smaller round hat underneath.

Jeremiah Hush was a bit puzzled by this, but thought it must be part of a P.I.'s normal appearance and procedures. Besides, the intrusion into his home was foremost on his mind. He told Winchester Bone about the strange disappearance of his umbrella and explained how, since that event, he didn't feel quite as peaceful in his own home.

Winchester Bone listened, nodded his head sympathetically, while chewing on the milk bone, switching it from one corner of his mouth to the other. When Jeremiah Hush finished talking, Win-

chester Bone took out a small round box from his breast pocket, put the bone carefully into it, and replaced the box in his pocket. He withdrew a small flat box from another pocket and took a pinch of red powder, sniffed it, then sneezed.

"Seventy-four percent paprika, twenty-three percent catnip, and three percent red pepper," he explained, "excellent for sinuses. Increases my sense of smell by forty-three and a half percent. That's important in my job." He sneezed again.

His large mustache fell off, revealing a mustache of more modest proportions underneath.

A well-seasoned P.I. Full of surprises and full of disguises, thought Jeremiah Hush, but he seems rather pleasant.

❡ Jeremiah Hush showed Winchester Bone his house. The P.I. looked around with great care, walking with difficulty, stopping periodically to sniff in all directions. His forehead was moist with sweat, so he took off his cape, to reveal a topcoat with a heavy lining underneath.

Winchester Bone scrupulously sniffed in all the places where Jeremiah Hush might have last left his umbrella. He wiped his forehead and took off his topcoat, growing noticeably thinner, and revealing a tweed jacket, worn out at the elbows. He resumed his investigation.

Finally Winchester Bone said, "Since the umbrella has only one leg, I mean, one handle, it's unlikely that it walked away by itself. Therefore, someone must've taken it. But who? That is the question. And where? is another. That someone must have some use for it."

"I suppose so," said Jeremiah Hush, who was beginning to get hungry.

"This isn't going to be an easy case," said Winchester Bone. "It can't be resolved today."

"It's late," said Jeremiah Hush. "Why don't you stay for supper."

"I never turn down a friendly invitation," said Winchester Bone.


⟮ After supper, they sat in the living room by the warm fireplace. Winchester Bone proposed a game of chess.

"There's nothing like a good bone and a good game of chess to stimulate the brain," he said, and took out his milk bone. The fire was warm. Winchester Bone took off his jacket. Now, in his striped vest, he sat comfortably in the soft chair. It was still hot, so he removed his thin mustache. Then, in order to see the game better, he took off his dark glasses, revealing slightly sad eyes.

Now the heavyset private investigator turned out to be a rather slender little Skye terrier, for Winchester Bone had also taken off his platform shoes with soles on springs, which gave him that wobbly walk and an additional two inches.

Jeremiah Hush was fascinated. He was beginning to like him and wasn't too concerned how good a P.I. he was.

Winchester Bone won the chess game and apologized, blaming it on luck.

Then, leaning back in his chair, he said: "My folks are descendants of the legendary Daniel-the-Riddle-Solver, who lived in the fourth century B.C. The famous private detective Sherlock Bone was my paternal great-great-great-grandfather. Brian D. Brain, my sixty-fifth cousin, wrote the definitive *Encyclopedia of Riddles and Puzzles*. I'm the youngest and smallest of my sixteen brothers and five sisters. My name, Winchester, is the longest, though. My brothers arc all P.I.s and work for the family business."

After a sip of hot cocoa, he continued: "Being the youngest and smallest, my brothers teased me a lot and made fun of me. So when the time came to join the family business, I decided to go off on my own. I knew it wouldn't be easy, but I love adventure."

"I don't care much for adventure," said Jeremiah Hush, "although I'm a descendant of C. Runoz de Noserac. He went to the moon in the seventeenth century, you know. He was famous for his nose, sword, and poetry. But I inherited only his nose and his love of poetry.

"I *love* my home. How can I enjoy it away on adventures? I love trees, but have never been much interested in family trees. Except for C. Runoz de Noserac, one branch of our family produced fruits, another nuts, if you know what I mean. The two never seem to agree with each other. And as far as roots are concerned, they're best kept underground where they belong, if you ask me."

They fell silent. Outside, it was raining hard.

"It's good for the trees," said Jeremiah Hush,

"but this is no night for driving; you're welcome to stay in the guest room."

"I'll give up the adventure of driving in the rain regretfully," said Winchester Bone, "but your offer is gratefully accepted. I'll get some sleep and resume the investigation tomorrow."

"The investigation? Why, of course," said Jeremiah Hush, who wasn't thinking of it just now but of how he had enjoyed the evening.

Winchester went to the guest room, put his bone under the pillow, and fell asleep immediately.

Jeremiah Hush went to his room. Lying in bed, he watched in his mind the day's events unfolding like a luminous movie that grew dimmer as he gradually sank into sleep.


( "Tunnel," said Winchester Bone, when he saw Jeremiah Hush in the kitchen the next morning.

"Huh?" asked Jeremiah Hush.

"There must be a tunnel in this house," said Winchester Bone.

"*A tunnel*? Utterly impossible."

"Are you quite sure?"

"Positive," said Jeremiah Hush, "I've lived here for sixteen years and know of no tunnel. What gave you such an idea?"

"I've developed a scientific guessing method," explained Winchester Bone over breakfast. "This method, when applied with great care and a pinch of luck, sometimes works."

He took out of one of his hidden pockets a small portable dictionary. "You see, eyes closed, I picked the letter T. I went through words beginning with T: tung, Tungus, Tungusic, tunic, tunicate, tunicle, tuning fork, tuning pipe. When I came to tunnel, I had a hunch and my nose twitched. Good sign: my nose knows. Do you have a basement?"

"Yes."

"Let's go down."


❪ "I just remembered something," said Jeremiah Hush. "I never leave my umbrella here. But on that rainy day, my umbrella was dripping all over the floor. I came down here to get a mop. I took the mop and left the umbrella to dry."

"Where?"

"Can't remember the exact spot," said Jeremiah Hush, "somewhere near the stairs, I think."

Under the basement stairs, where it was darkest, they felt a faint draft of cool air coming from behind an empty barrel and wooden boards leaning against the wall. When they moved the barrel and the wood, Jeremiah Hush directed his flashlight to that spot, and they saw an opening in the wall.

"The tunnel," said Winchester Bone triumphantly.

*"Ten thousand monkeys and an elephant!"* exclaimed Jeremiah Hush. "How in the world did you figure it out?"

"Simplicity itself, my dear Mr. Hush. A hunch confirmed by sniffing developed almost to a science, and all reinforced by intuition."

"I don't fully understand it," said Jeremiah Hush.

"Neither do I, but let's find out where the tunnel leads."

¶ To enter the pitch-dark tunnel, they had to crawl. Gradually it became large enough for them to stand up. As they advanced, Jeremiah Hush's flashlight revealed rocks and roots in the long, twisting, turning, underground passageway.

"Chilly," said Jeremiah Hush.

"Damp, too," said Winchester Bone.

After a long walk, the twisting tunnel split in two. Winchester Bone sniffed in both directions and headed to the right, followed by Jeremiah Hush. They walked for some time, until they came to another fork. This time they headed left.

Jeremiah Hush's flashlight was growing dimmer. "The battery is dying," he said. "We'd better save it for emergencies." Now they continued in total darkness, guided by Winchester Bone's sense of smell, and by feeling the walls as they walked. This was becoming more of an adventure than Jeremiah Hush cared to have between breakfast and lunch. He didn't know if they were near to or far from his basement. Breakfast certainly felt very far away.

"I miss home," said Jeremiah Hush.

"But you are home," said Winchester Bone.

"It doesn't feel like home," said Jeremiah Hush.

"We might have been walking in circles, for all we know," said Winchester Bone.

"I can't tell one passageway from another," said Jeremiah Hush. "Just imagine, a maze of secret passageways right under my own house."

"Sometimes we don't know what's under our own nose—or above it, for that matter," said Winchester Bone. "I once saw a picture of a brain. It looked like a maze. I could easily get lost in the labyrinth of my own brain."

❡ They continued on their way in the dark, proceeding cautiously so as not to trip over the occasional protruding roots.

Jeremiah Hush shivered. He was chilly, hungry, and a bit scared.

"Wait," said Winchester Bone, sniffing vigorously.

"What?" asked Jeremiah Hush, perking up.

"I'm not sure yet, but I'm picking something up, just ahead."

When they came out of the next turn, the tunnel seemed to be less dark. Walking faster, they reached a thin strip of light on the ground, coming from under a door. Jeremiah Hush lit his flashlight, and they saw a small sign:

ARCHIBALD METHUSELAH, JR.

They knocked. No answer. They knocked louder. Still no reply. After waiting a while, they tried the door. It wasn't locked but it made a loud creaking sound as it opened. They entered.

The room was dim, lit only by the light from the stove. A large, steaming teakettle was casting an enormous shadow on the wall. The flickering light from the stove highlighted a small table, a couple of stools, and a portion of a small cabinet.

"I hear footsteps," whispered Winchester Bone.

The shuffling of feet came closer. Then a loud "Atchooo!" A door opened and a shadow appeared. Slightly bent, cane in hand, dragging one foot, the shadow moved slowly toward the stove. They saw the dimly lit features of an old woodchuck with a white beard, wearing a long robe. "Atchoo!" he sneezed, almost extinguishing the flame. He took out a handkerchief and blew his nose loudly, while mumbling something to himself.

"Sir," said Winchester Bone, "excuse us for entering . . ."

But the old woodchuck paid no attention and acted as if they weren't there.

"Excuse us," said Jeremiah Hush, louder. No response. The woodchuck brought the teakettle to the table, mumbling to himself.

"Sir!" said Winchester Bone, very loud.

The woodchuck stopped, looked around the room, then resumed pouring tea into a cup. Jeremiah Hush and Winchester Bone looked at each other, puzzled. The woodchuck shuffled back and forth, ignoring them

"Halloo, sir!" shouted Winchester Bone.

"Huh?" mumbled the woodchuck. "Could've sworn I heard something." And he sneezed again.

"Sir!" called out Jeremiah Hush and Winchester Bone together.

"Huh? Did I hear something?" the woodchuck said, and put his paw to his ear. "Speak up, don't whisper!"

"Yes! You did!" shouted Jeremiah Hush and Winchester Bone together at the top of their voices. "Can we talk to you?"

"Ah, visitors!" shouted the woodchuck with relief. "Glad I wasn't imagining. Howdy! Don't leave! Be right back!"

He shuffled out of the room and came back with a large horn, which he put to his ear.

"I'm a trifle hard of hearing," he explained in a very loud voice.

"Can you hear me?" asked Jeremiah Hush.

"Yup!" shouted the woodchuck, "just right."

"It is Mr. Methuselah, isn't it?" asked Winchester Bone.

"Archibald Methuselah, Jr., sure is. Do I know you?" he said in his shouting voice.

"No, I'm Jeremiah Hush. We apologize for entering like this. We are lost. We knocked at your door, but there was no answer."

"Quite all right," said Mr. Methuselah between sneezes. "You're just in time for tea. I'll get a couple of cups. Since I retired, I don't get many visitors."

They sat sipping hot tea and eating toast with peanut butter. Jeremiah Hush felt warmth return to his body. "Thanks for the hot tea," he said.

"You bet. Hot tea's just right. Gets out the chill," said Mr. Methuselah. "Had this cold for days now and can't shake it off!" He sneezed, then continued: "I'm a retired mushroom farmer. My eyes have never been good. Now I can't see too much and had to give up farming. That's why I don't use lights. My hearing isn't too good either. Glad you fellows dropped by. What's your names, you said?"

"Jeremiah Hush. I live upstairs, in the house."

"House?" said Mr. Methuselah, surprised. "Lived here all my life and never heard of any house."

"I'm Winchester Bone, P.I., investigating a missing umbrella."

"Huh? Umbrella?" said Mr. Methuselah.

Jeremiah Hush told him about the disappearance of his umbrella and their search for it.

"Ten thousand toadstools on a tree trunk!" said Mr. Methuselah. "That umbrella! Must've been your umbrella, then! Racked my brain for days trying to figure out whose umbrella it was."

"I'm glad you have it," said Jeremiah Hush.

"Trouble is, I don't," said Mr. Methuselah. "Last week I put a touch of brandy in my tea, for my cold. It might've been a touch too much! I was going about, sniffing and sneezing, I was a bit dizzy, too. I was looking for my cane, wandering in the hallways, and must've gotten to the emergency exit. Never been there before. Had to crawl out between wood planks, then bumped into a barrel. There I got hold of my cane handle."

"Emergency exit in my basement?" said Jeremiah Hush.

"Huh?" said Mr. Methuselah, and continued: "When I got home and felt the rest of it, I knew for sure it wasn't my cane. It was an umbrella. But whose?"

"Where is it?" asked Winchester Bone.

"I gave it to Akbar. I didn't know what else to do."

"Who's that?"

"My neighbor, Akbar von Mousenhousen. He collects everything. Let's go see him."

([There's a long way and there's a short way. Mr. Methuselah knew the short way by heart, and although he walked slowly, he got them through the maze of hallways in no time. He rang a doorbell. Then he rang several more times before they heard a faint click, as if someone was watching through the peephole. Finally a voice said, "Who's there?"

"Huh?" said Mr. Methuselah, "huh?" and he sneezed.

"Archie, is that you?"

"You bet! Open up!"

The door opened a crack, and a thin twitching nose with long whiskers poked out and sniffed left and right. The door opened some more, revealing a mouse with a long, thin face and small eyes, wearing a monocle and a wrinkled cap.

"It is you, Archie," said Akbar von Mousenhousen. He cautiously opened the door with nervous little movements. Through the partially open door, Jeremiah Hush and Winchester Bone saw that the room behind was packed from wall to wall, and from floor to ceiling, with objects of all shapes, sizes, and descriptions. "Who are they?"

Mr. Methuselah introduced Jeremiah Hush and Winchester Bone, and explained why they were there.

"Show them the umbrella I gave you," he said.

"I gave it away," said Akbar von Mousenhousen.

"Gave it away?" asked Mr. Methuselah, surprised. "You?"

"Couldn't help it, Archie," apologized Akbar

von Mousenhousen. "'Twas my forty-sixth cousin-in-law's birthday. I had to give him something, and had no time to find another present. Thought you wouldn't mind. Dreadfully sorry."

"Where does he live?" asked Winchester Bone.

"Upstairs."

*"Upstairs?"* said Jeremiah Hush. "Where upstairs?"

"Take them to him, Akbar!" said Mr. Methuselah.

"Sure," said Akbar von Mousenhousen.

Jeremiah Hush and Winchester Bone thanked Mr. Methuselah for his help.

"Stop by to visit," said he. "I've got lots of time and few visitors!"

⟨ After getting out of the tunnel through another well-hidden exit, they followed Akbar von Mousenhousen along a narrow path overhung with vegetation, through which, from time to time, they saw small patches of sky.

"My distant cousin is a hard bird to find."

"Bird?" said Jeremiah Hush.

"I mean, owl," explained Akbar von Mousenhousen. "He used to be married to the thirty-seventh niece of my forty-fifth great-great-aunt Mildred."

Jeremiah Hush was surprised to see that they were now near his house. They had approached at an angle, from a direction he never walked in, creature of habit that he was. They were at the back end of the house, hidden from the road and shaded by the big old oak tree. Von Mousenhousen climbed the tree on ladder-like steps, followed by Jeremiah Hush and Winchester Bone. They reached a small wooden platform invisible from the ground because of thick branches. It was level with a small round window in the attic of the house. Akbar von Mousenhousen pulled on a thick laundry rope on pulleys, extending to the attic window. "He doesn't believe in teleblablaphones," he said. Several clothespins hanging on the rope reached them. One of these held a note on a card: "Out for the evening. Come back tomorrow morning. O.O."

"Didn't I tell you?" said Akbar von Mousenhousen. "He's out a lot and he's full of surprises. I must get back now. Good luck."

"Surprises?" said Winchester Bone. "I like

that." Turning to Jeremiah, he asked, "Are you ready to give up?"

"No, never," said Jeremiah Hush. "I must know what happened to my umbrella. Otherwise I'll always feel unsettled in my own house."

( Next morning they were back. When they pulled the laundry rope, a note on one of the clothespins said: "Congratulations. I'm home. Keep pulling. O.O." So they did. Another note arrived the same way; it said: "But need more sleep. Pull. O.O." The next one said: "Solve the riddles. While you solve, I catch up on my sleep. Pull. O.O."

They were intrigued. The last note said: *"1. It stands on one leg but never gets tired and goes nowhere but up. 2. Red, blue, or yellow. Any color pick. Cozy walk, my fellow. A ceiling on a stick.* What is it? Have fun. O.O."

"Hmm, interesting," said Winchester Bone, who couldn't pass up a riddle.

"Let's go and think about it over a cup of hot cocoa," suggested Jeremiah Hush, who couldn't pass up a cup of hot cocoa.

They joined forces, thought hard, discussed it,

then returned to the tree deck. Winchester Bone wrote on the card: *"1. Mushroom."* Jeremiah Hush wrote: *"2. Umbrella."* After a moment a note arrived. It said: "Passed. Hope didn't tire you. I'm rested. Coming. O.O."

Shortly after, a middle aged owl with thick eyeglasses came riding over in a basket hanging from the rope. He called, "Howdy," and jumped on the deck. He was wearing a top hat, a wrinkled black evening coat with tails, and no shoes.

"Sorry to have kept you waiting, old fellows," he said. "Late to bed and late to rise, keeps me calm, rested, and wise, if you'll forgive my poor rhyme. I'm Obadiah Ooh. I live upstairs, in the attic."

"I'm Jeremiah Hush, I live downstairs."

"And I'm Winchester Bone, P.I., working on a case."

"Case," said Obadiah Ooh. "Mystery, something dim, misty, dark, shrouded in shadows. Terrific! I'm a night person, remember? Tell me all about it."

Jeremiah Hush told him about his missing umbrella, and Winchester Bone filled in the details of their search.

"I wish I'd known it was your umbrella," said O.O. "When Akbar gave it to me, it already had two holes in it. Th... punctured on the tree b

"Rain clou ... said Jeremiah Hush, ... ver know the end of it.

"Sorry, old ... find your umbrella, I p... cket and hat, and put th ... r action. See you soon."

[Jeremiah Hu ... r Bone that he might as ... tion of the investigation

By the next da ... up on Obadiah Ooh, w ... rang.

"Follow me, old fellows," said Obadiah Ooh with an air of intrigue.

He led them to the back of the house, then down a hill, among trees, through thick bushes and grass, to a narrow winding path that led to a pond. They came to a small hill and a modest sign, P. S. BEAVER, ARCHITECT. When they reached

the top, they saw, partly hidden, a house. But no ordinary house.

It was imbedded in the hill, as if growing out of it. The roof was built from an overturned boat shell, and its sides had windows made up of small pieces of glass, which reflected the sunlight in a rainbow of colors. On top of the roof was a tower, with clear, round windows. The house seemed to have been built of found materials, stones, branches, old cans, empty bottles, and other odd-shaped objects. They were all put together in the most imaginative and unexpected ways, and united into a pleasing whole.

Jeremiah Hush was astounded.

"Where are we?" he asked O.O.

"We're right near your house," explained O.O., who knew the territory from a bird's-eye view. "It seems far because of the circular path, and you couldn't see it because it's hidden by the hill and the trees."


( [ Obadiah Ooh rang the doorbell. A young beaver opened the door. Her hair was gathered into a bun in the back, and she wore a carpenter's multipocketed apron, filled with pencils, rulers, and tools, over her long skirt.

"We're looking for Mr. P. S. Beaver, architect," said O.O.

"I'm she," she said.

❨ After an initial moment of surprise, O.O. explained that while flying low over her house he saw something resembling the umbrella he'd thrown out. Jeremiah Hush filled in the rest.

P.S. took them to the back of the house and to an unfinished round porch. In the center of the roof was an umbrella-shaped dome, with openings filled with pieces of glass that cast multicolored reflections on the floor.

"Was this your umbrella, Mr. Hush?" asked P.S., pointing to the center of the porch roof.

"Yes, it was," said Jeremiah Hush, who had climbed a ladder to get a closer look. "I can still see the partly worn-out *JH* I had carved on the tip of its handle when I bought it."

"I found it a couple of days ago, floating down the stream," said P.S. "It was full of holes, but I'll dismantle the roof and return it to you, if you wish."

"Oh, no," said Jeremiah Hush, horrified. "Please don't. Sooner or later my umbrella would've collapsed and died, but here it has found a happy home and will be forever a part of your house. And you've found an admirer of your architecture."

"Two admirers," said Winchester Bone.

"Three," said Obadiah Ooh. "Don't leave me out."

"A friend of my work is a friend of mine," said P.S. "You've found yourselves a friend."


"I'm all packed and ready to go," said Winchester Bone.

"What do I owe you for your services?"

"My dear Jeremiah Hush, I'm afraid I haven't actually recovered your umbrella. You provided me with room and board, not to mention your incomparable hot cocoa, and the pleasure of the investigation and of your company and of meeting your neighbors. In short, some of the most delightful days of my young career. You owe me nothing."

"I'm sorry to see you go," said Jeremiah Hush. "If it weren't for you and my lost umbrella, I wouldn't have had this adventure, which in spite of myself I've enjoyed. I wouldn't have known I had neighbors, let alone become friends with them. This is well worth three umbrellas, at the very least, not to mention another new friend, you, if you don't mind my saying so."

"Likewise, my dear Jeremiah Hush, likewise."

The front doorbell rang. When Jeremiah Hush opened the door, no one was there, but there was a long, narrow package with his name on it. He opened it and found a brand-new umbrella and a note:

To: *Jeremiah Hush*
From: *Those responsible for the loss of your umbrella*
Contents: *Replacement umbrella*
Purpose: *Apologies, and to keep you dry, and to invite you to a picnic*
When: *Tomorrow*
Where: *Pond*

Why: *First day of spring and to enjoy new friends and neighbors*
Requirements: *Jeremiah Hush and Winchester Bone in attendance*
Signed: *Archie Methuselah, Akbar von Mousenhousen, Obadiah Ooh, P.S. Beaver*

"Well, Winchester Bone, for an ending it is a good ending, isn't it?"

"Yes, indeed," said Winchester Bone.

"And now, my friend, set your bags down and pull up a chair. We'll have a game of chess and hot cocoa, for of course you cannot leave until the picnic is over," concluded Jeremiah Hush.

# Jeremiah Hush Goes to the Fair

BEING A FAIRLY
DETAILED ACCOUNT IN
WHICH IT IS CLEARLY SHOWN
HOW CONSUMING FOUR CHOCOLATE-
BANANA-PECAN CREAM PIES INSTEAD
OF BREAKFAST CAN LEAD TO
THE MOST UNEXPECTED
CONSEQUENCES

❡ The doorbell rang.

"Good morning, my friend," said Winchester Bone, bright and cheerful, when Jeremiah Hush, in terry-cloth robe and slippers, slowly opened the front door. "Good morning, we're going out."

"We are?" said Jeremiah Hush, trying unsuccessfully to suppress a yawn.

"Come, let's go to the fair," said Winchester Bone.

"The fair?" said Jeremiah Hush sleepily. "What fair?"

"You know, the fair in Orangutanville. Magicians, musicians, performers, exhibits, competitions, food—the fair," said Winchester Bone, as he followed Jeremiah Hush into the house. "How can you stay at home?"

"I can," said Jeremiah Hush, closing one eye.

"And miss all the fun?"

"Fun?" said Jeremiah Hush, making a brave effort to keep the other eye open.

"The pie-eating contest?"

"*Pie!* What kind of pie?"

"Oh, nothing fancy," said Winchester Bone, "just chocolate-banana-pecan cream pie. But never mind."

"*Chocolate-banana-pecan cream pie!*" repeated Jeremiah Hush slowly, weighing every word and opening both eyes. "My favorite. Why didn't you say so? I'm going. But what about breakfast?"

"We haven't got time."

"All right, I'm coming," said Jeremiah Hush,

and went with great effort to his room upstairs, while Winchester Bone settled on the couch in the living room.

When our hero returned all dressed, Winchester Bone got up and said, "Let's go."

"Not yet. Be right back."

"Now what?"

"I go without breakfast, but I don't go without saying goodbye to my friends."

"Friends?"

"Yes. You know, my trees, pond, frogs, birds, crickets," said Jeremiah Hush.

"But you'll be back in no time."

"One never knows," said our hero philosophically. "Be it a long or a short absence, who knows when I'll be back? I always say goodbye to my old friends before a trip. I'll miss them. Besides, it's good luck."

When Jeremiah Hush returned, Winchester Bone said, "I've invited Obadiah Ooh, Archibald Methuselah, Jr., Akbar von Mousenhousen, and P. S. Beaver to join us. They'll be coming along later and will meet us at the fair."

"Great idea," agreed Jeremiah. "Why didn't I think of that?"

⟨A benevolent sun playfully tickled the tree leaves, caressed the rolling hills, touched the curving road here and there. Winchester Bone sat at the wheel, steering his autodrivemobile toward Orangutanville, while Jeremiah Hush, a broad smile on his face, was in the back taking a nap and dreaming of a parade of creamy chocolate-banana-pecan pies.

From a distance, the fair was an array of movement, shapes, colors, and terrific noises. When they got closer, they saw merchants and peddlers displaying their wares, sellers of nostrums, buyers, strollers, and onlookers. They struggled through crowds watching entertainers of all kinds, freak shows, tumblers, and conjurers. They stopped briefly to see brightly dressed clowns on stilts and acrobats turning hoops. They squeezed through thick crowds to watch contortionists tying themselves into knots, then untying themselves. A little farther on, jugglers juggled burning torches, while other performers swallowed swords, then fire. The sounds of singers and musicians, rattles and drums, reached their ears, but they couldn't get close enough to see them. They passed by amusement booths, stalls, and puppet shows.

"Watch your wallet," whispered Winchester Bone to Jeremiah Hush. Among the thick crowds, there were also pickpockets.

A light breeze carried the smells of foods. Odors of stewed, dried, and raw fruits, different kinds of nuts, spiced soups, a variety of exotic dishes, and delicious pies tickled the nostrils of our starving hero. "I can't wait to get to the pies," he said to Winchester Bone.


❨In front of a huge tent that had a long, colorful sign, PIE-EATING CONTEST, a crowd was admiring an exquisite display of chocolate-banana-pecan cream pies.

"Oh, wonder of pies," said Jeremiah Hush to his friend, when they had squeezed through the crowd and were able to look at the pie. "My mouth is watering and my stomach is growling."

A giraffe in a colorful outfit stood on a stool and called above the hustle and bustle: *"Come one, come all!* You of strong appetite and discriminating taste buds! Test your chewing powers and

swallowing valor! Come compete in the greatest of all pie-eating contests! Come savor the unbelievable delights of the world's most delicious chocolate-banana-pecan cream pies! Come win the one-thousand-banana prize! We are honored to have as our special participant and challenger the greatest pie-eating champion of all time, magician of pie eaters, the incomparable, the invincible, the unique, the one and only—Fffreddie Fffoxxx! *Come one, come all!*"

Jeremiah Hush and Winchester Bone followed the large crowd into the tent. Inside was a long, wide table with chairs on both sides; some contestants were already seated. The crowd sat on rows of benches around the table and by the tent walls. Our friends sat down in the first row, close to the table.

"We need more contestants," called the giraffe. "How about it, ladies and gentlemen!"

"How about it?" Jeremiah Hush asked his friend.

"Not me," said Winchester Bone. "I couldn't finish a single pie. Besides, I've had a big breakfast. How about you? Aren't you hungry?"

"Sta                              . And he got up
to join

([Th                              for the pie-eating
cha                             incomparable, the
uni                             The audience was
tal                             iah closed his eyes
an                              ith a huge, bottom-
les                            outh, whose hunger
for pies could nev            ed. He got scared. He
thought he might have been too hasty in jumping
into the contest, and perhaps he should quit while
there still was time. While he was debating what
to do, he heard the giraffe call: Ladies and gentlemen, here's the great, the one and only Fffreddie
Fffoxxx!!!"

Silence. Then thunderous applause, as the champion made his entrance and sat down by the table.
Jeremiah Hush opened his eyes. Seated across from
him was a slight, slim, short fellow of a fox in a
large, wide-brim hat, with a pointed nose, yellow-
ish complexion, tight mouth, and hungry, fiery,
little eyes.

"The contest will last one hour, with a ten-

minute break. Whoever can eat the most pies in the hour will be the winner," explained the giraffe. "And now, ladies and gentlemen, here are the pies!!!"

The smell of freshly baked pies invaded the tent, preceding the pie carriers, who came in and placed a pie on the table in front of each contestant. A bell rang. The contest began.

The audience was silent, respectfully listening to the vigorous chewing. They watched the contestants gobble, gulp, and devour one pie, then quickly reach for another.

Jeremiah Hush, cream all over his nose and around his mouth, was biting big chunks of pie and swallowing with gusto. From the corner of his eye he could see Winchester Bone, seated close by, watching the contest intently. While chewing, Jeremiah Hush glanced at the world champ. He saw Freddie Fox reach out with his left paw and grab a pie. He would bring it to his mouth somewhat nervously, quickly swallow sizable portions, wrinkle his forehead, and roll his eyes. From time to time, he scratched his cheek with his right paw.

His short, trimmed claws were covered with chocolate and cream.

Jeremiah Hush was doing fine, breakfastless as he was. In fact, so far he was only half a pie behind the world champ.

After the second pie, a few contestants bowed out. Jeremiah Hush kept chewing. But by the end of the third pie, he had slowed down. He wasn't as hungry anymore, but he did his best to catch up with Freddie Fox, who was also beginning to flag and was scratching his cheek more frequently, with jerky little movements.

Now Jeremiah Hush made a brave effort to swallow faster. Sweat was trickling down his forehead and into his mouth, adding a salty taste to the sweet pie. By the middle of the fourth pie, he was ahead of all the others, and only three bites behind the champion.

A bell rang.

"We'll have a ten-minute break," announced the giraffe.

Freddie Fox requested a breath of fresh air, and permission granted, he passed in front of Winchester Bone and left through the back exit. Jeremiah Hush noticed his friend wrinkling his nose, and a moment later, when Jeremiah Hush looked for Winchester, he didn't see him.

Jeremiah sat back and gently massaged his belly, getting ready for the final run. Freddie Fox returned, walking briskly to his seat, holding the brim of his hat with his paw.

( After the break, Jeremiah Hush felt as if the pies were gradually expanding in his stomach like a big, heavy sponge. He was very slow now. But Freddie Fox was going stronger than ever, eating with a renewed appetite. Our hero was astonished. How could ten minutes make such a difference? he thought. Now he's devouring pies as if he fasted all week. Where in the world can all this food go in such a slight and slim fellow? Jeremiah felt stuffed, and discouraged, as he watched Freddie Fox eagerly reaching out with his left paw for his sixth pie, and patting his hat with his right paw, as if making sure it was still there.

Jeremiah Hush chewed automatically. He was the only runner-up, for everyone else had dropped

s fourth pie, he couldn't
ave up. He sat in amaze-
:d a seventh pie into his
emiah Hush wiped the
ose. The sharp claws of
ached out for another
:, but Jeremiah Hush
(                          as.

announced the giraffe.
............ encouragements to Freddie,
urging him to speed up and set a new record. Jeremiah Hush and Winchester Bone exchanged puzzled glances. Freddie Fox, his forehead wrinkled,
cream all over his nose and paws, kept swallowing
chunks of pie. When the final bell rang, he had
finished seven and a half pies. Everybody cheered.


( The giraffe motioned for silence as he prepared
to announce the winner. Just then Jeremiah Hush
figured out what was wrong, stood up, and called,
*"He's an impostor!"* Jeremiah Hush's normally
quiet friend, Winchester Bone, jumped on the
table, pointed at the winner, and called, *"Arrest
him!"*

Dead silence fell on the tent. Freddie Fox gave Winchester Bone a horrified look, glanced at Jeremiah Hush, and shrieked, "They're crazy!"

Pointing at Winchester Bone, someone called, "He's a friend of one of the losers!"

"Spoilsport!" shouted another.

After that, it was total chaos. Everybody went wild and began yelling all at once, shoving and pushing.

During the commotion, Freddie Fox disappeared. Our friends headed for the back exit. But this wasn't easy. They had to battle their way through the crowd until finally they were able to get out of the tent. Winchester Bone was first, followed by Jeremiah Hush, who was slower because he felt so heavy. They saw the fox in the distance and ran after him.

( Freddie Fox opened the door of an autodrive-mobile which had a small sign, F. N. FOX ENTERPRISES, printed on the door. Before he could close the door, Winchester Bone grabbed him from behind. While the private investigator struggled with the fox, the other door of the autodrivemobile opened and another, identical-looking Freddie Fox got out and rushed toward Winchester Bone.

Just then, Jeremiah Hush arrived. His heart was pounding, and his knees felt weak. But regardless, he tried as best he could to help his friend, and grabbed the second Freddie Fox from behind. Now the first Freddie Fox managed to release himself from Winchester Bone's grip and turn around, hissing in his face, a thin, but powerful *ffffff* sound, emitting the most foul bad breath imaginable right into Winchester Bone's sensitive nose. Winchester Bone grabbed his nose and howled.

Then Freddie Fox-1, leaving Winchester Bone behind, ran to the rescue of Freddie Fox-2, struggled with Jeremiah Hush, and began blowing his bad breath into our hero's face.

Jeremiah Hush couldn't withstand the foul smell and loosened his grip. Whereupon Freddie Fox-2 turned around and began spitting thin jets of well-aimed saliva at Jeremiah Hush's eyes.

They mustn't get away, thought Jeremiah and made an effort to keep his eyes open in spite of the strong burning sensation.

Jeremiah Hush saw the foxes escaping. He ran

after them, blinking his irritated eyes, trying not to lose sight of them.

In the meantime, Winchester Bone, who had sufficiently recovered, joined in the chase. But the distance between our friends and the foxes was widening.

Some onlookers were startled, others puzzled. Many were amused, thinking the chase was part of the fair routine. But nobody helped. Jeremiah Hush and Winchester Bone, battling to get through the crowd, could barely see the foxes. Suddenly they heard a voice they knew.

"Stop them! Stop them!" Archibald Methuselah shouted as he and their other friends, who had come late to the fair, joined the chase. Obadiah Ooh flew over the thick crowds, guiding the pursuers to the foxes, while Akbar von Mousenhousen ran between the feet of the onlookers. P.S., Jeremiah Hush, and Winchester Bone pushed their way through the crowds as fast as they could.


❪While the commotion in the tent was going on, the giraffe had called the Orangutanville County Watchdog Security Office.

Just after our five friends managed to corner the foxes, making sure they couldn't run away, the officers arrived.

"You give Orangutanville County a bad reputation," said one officer as he put handcuffs on the first Freddie Fox.

"Shame on you," said another officer, arresting the second Freddie Fox. "Today a pie, tomorrow a bakery, eh?"

In the meantime, curious onlookers had gathered around. Some of them were from the pie-eating crowd.

A dignified gentleman fox approached the twins and said, "You're a disgrace to all creatures of the fox persuasion," and walked away, indignant.

The giraffe came over, an expression of disbelief on his face. "What does it mean," he said, "two Freddie Foxes?"

"Identical twins," explained Sergeant Moose. "They have a long criminal record. His real name is Carl Lemon. And this one is Clarence Lemon," he said, pointing to the other Freddie Fox.

"No," said the first Freddie Fox, "it's the other way around."

"No," said the other Freddie Fox. "I'm Carl and he's Clarence."

"Never mind," said Sergeant Moose. "Just listening to you gives me a headache."

A lady collie came over and said to the Lemon brothers, "I'm Laura-Lee Lemon, of Lemon, Lemon, and Lemon, Unlimited. How dare you stain the Lemon reputation! You ought to be ashamed of yourselves!" and walked away.

Sergeant Moose turned to Jeremiah Hush, Winchester Bone, and their friends. "There's a fifteen-hundred-banana reward for their capture. Stop by tomorrow at the station to pick it up, won't you?" Then, confronting the twins, he said, "Off to jail, both of you!"

And off they went.


( The giraffe turned to Jeremiah Hush and Winchester Bone, and said, "I owe you a great debt. If it weren't for you, the first prize would've gone to a crook . . . that is, crooks. Identical twins, hah! I can't get over it." Then he said to Jeremiah Hush, "That makes you the winner, doesn't it?

You did extremely well against the two Foxes; I mean, the Lemon brothers."

The crowd cheered as he handed our hero a check for a thousand bananas. Some came over to congratulate him while others apologized to him and to Winchester Bone, and praised them for what they had done.

Meanwhile, Akbar von Mousenhousen went to get Archibald Methuselah, Jr., who hadn't been able to keep up in the race because of his age. When he returned with the old woodchuck, Archibald said in his usual way . . . that is, shouting at the top of his lungs, "Tell me all about it!" and the others joined in, asking how Jeremiah and Winchester had seen through the hoax. Our friends couldn't hold back their excitement any longer.

"Simplicity itself," said Winchester Bone, "thanks to Jeremiah Hush."

"No," said Jeremiah Hush, "thanks to you."

"Explain," said P.S.

"You begin," said Jeremiah Hush to Winchester Bone.

"Very well." The private investigator chewed on his bone. "After Jeremiah had joined the contestants, I picked a spot where I could watch the 'champ' closely. Professional curiosity, you see. Something didn't smell right to me."

"What didn't smell right?" asked Akbar von Mousenhousen.

"Couldn't tell," said Winchester Bone, "not at first, anyway. For one thing, I got a whiff of his unnatural breath. You see, my nose knows. It's sensitive. Never smelled this type of smell before."

"From the start I, too, had a funny feeling about him," said Jeremiah Hush. "I'd expected the champ to look different. I was disappointed when I saw him, but I was also relieved that he wasn't as big as I had feared. But the peculiar rolling of his eyes from side to side aroused my suspicion."

"Good for you," said Winchester Bone.

"I kept watching him," Jeremiah continued, "and I noticed that the claws on his right paw— the one that kept reaching for the pies—were rather short."

"Go on," said Obadiah.

"But after the break," said Jeremiah Hush, "the claws on that paw were much longer. Now, claws can be clipped in a hurry, but cannot grow back in ten minutes. Don't you agree, Winchester?"

"Certainly," said Winchester Bone.

"Good thinking," said P.S.

Jeremiah Hush smiled at her and went on: "His renewed appetite after the break didn't sit right with me, either."

"You bet!" shouted Mr. Methuselah.

"And another thing," said Winchester Bone; "before the break he was always scratching his cheek. After the break, though, he kept patting his hat. It looked to me like an old habit of his, not just a coincidence, unlikely to have changed in ten minutes. Don't you agree, Jeremiah?"

"Indeed, I do."

"Then what?" said Obadiah.

"When I didn't see Winchester during the break," said Jeremiah Hush, "I figured he'd followed Freddie Fox."

"What did you see?" P.S. asked Winchester Bone.

"I saw him approach an autodrivemobile parked nearby," said Winchester Bone, "enter through one door, walk out the other, and then head back to the tent. All he did was pass through the car. Peculiar way of catching a breath of fresh air during a ten-minute break, if you ask me."

"Hah, some breath of fresh air!" said Akbar von Mousenhousen.

"Another thing," continued the private investigator. "During the contest, Freddie Fox wrinkled his forehead, which indicated he wasn't wearing a mask. I know a thing or two about disguises."

Jeremiah Hush smiled at Winchester Bone. "You're the master," he said. "So, since Freddie Fox's mannerisms had changed drastically in ten minutes, it became clear that we were dealing with identical twins . . ."

". . . who had switched places during the break . . ." said Winchester Bone.

". . . and I was facing, not one, but two competitors," finished Jeremiah Hush.

"What you fellows did," said Obadiah, "is nothing short of *brilliant!*"

"Team work, my dear Obadiah," said Winchester.

"All we did was put two and two together," said Jeremiah.

Then Winchester Bone turned to Jeremiah Hush and said, "For someone who dislikes adventures, you did pretty well, my friend."

"Adventures are all right," said Jeremiah Hush, "once every seven and a half months. But never after a huge breakfast."

They looked at one another and burst out laughing. And everybody joined in.